W9-AXY-287

BLAZE SHOWS
THE WAY

BLAZE SHOWS THE WAY

Story and Pictures by C. W. ANDERSON

Aladdin Paperbacks

Revised Cover Edition, 2000
Aladdin Paperbacks
An imprint of Simon & Schuster Children's Publishing Division
1230 Avenue of the Americas, New York, NY 10020
Copyright © 1969 by C. W. Anderson
First Aladdin Paperbacks edition, 1994

Printed in the United States of America
20 19 18 17 16 15 14 13 12 11

Library of Congress Cataloging-in-Publication Data
Anderson, C. W. (Clarence William), date.
Blaze shows the way : Billy and Blaze help a friend. Story and pictures / by C. W. Anderson.
— 1st Aladdin Books ed.
p.   cm.
Summary: Billy and his friend Tommy enter their ponies in the pair jumping contest.
ISBN 0-689-71776-8
[1. Horses—Fiction.]   I. Title.
[PZ7.A524Bp   1994]

[E]—dc20   93-1454

To Craig
and his pony, Simbal

Billy was a boy who had a pony named Blaze that he loved very much. Billy was a good friend of Tommy, who lived next door. Tommy had a little gray spotted pony named Dusty. Blaze and Dusty were also very good friends.

Tommy learned from Billy how to take care of his pony and keep him clean so that his coat always shone as Blaze's did. Tommy wanted Dusty to be like Blaze, for he thought Blaze was the finest pony in the world.

When the boys went riding together, Tommy always watched Billy and tried to ride just the way he did. Billy and Blaze had won a beautiful silver cup at a horse show, and Tommy hoped that someday he and Dusty could ride in a show and win a prize.

Sometimes on their rides through the woods they would come to a tree that had fallen across the path. Then Blaze seemed happy, for he loved to jump and so did Billy.

But Dusty always stopped in front of the tree and would not jump.

Then Billy and Blaze had to stop, too, and come
back and wait while Tommy tried to find a
way around the tree.

"Maybe Dusty once hurt himself jumping," said Billy, "and now he's afraid." Tommy thought that might be so, but still he was sad that Dusty would not jump like Blaze.

One day when they were out riding they saw a
sign announcing a horse show the next day.
"Pony Class—Jumping in Pairs," read Billy.
"First prize—two silver cups."

"What is jumping in pairs?" asked Tommy.
"Two ponies jumping side by side," said Billy.
"If only Dusty would jump we could try for
that," said Tommy. "How I wish Dusty could
win a silver cup."

They had not gone far when Billy suddenly called "Whoa!" to Blaze. "Look how black that cloud is," he said. "There must be a big storm coming. Let's hurry home." Then the wind began to blow. It whistled through the trees.

Both ponies started for home at a gallop. When there was a bright flash of lightning and a sharp clap of thunder, they went even faster. They did not like the storm and wanted to be safely in their stables.

Suddenly Billy saw that a tree had been blown down right across the path! He tried to stop Blaze, for he knew Dusty would not jump. But Blaze was frightened and kept going faster. So did Dusty.

Both ponies jumped together and were over and galloping fast. "He jumped!" cried Tommy. "Dusty jumped!" Tommy was very happy, and Dusty seemed happy, too.

Just before they came out of the woods they
saw another tree that had blown down. Billy was
worried that this time Dusty would not jump.
But again, he jumped right along with Blaze.

Soon they were near home. "What a storm!" shouted Billy. "But now we're safe."

After Billy had taken care of Blaze he helped Tommy rub down Dusty until he was all dry. "Dusty jumped wonderfully," said Tommy. "Maybe now we can ride in the horse show." "Well," said Billy, "it's tomorrow, and we really should have more time to practice. But we can try."

The next day the sky was blue and the sun was bright. Billy and Tommy worked hard. Both ponies looked beautiful with their shining coats and their silky manes and tails. "Remember," said Billy, "our ponies must jump side by side to win."

"I'm sure they will," said Tommy. "Dusty always wants to be right beside Blaze."

The first ponies that jumped did not keep side
by side. All the way around the ring one was
far ahead of the other.

40

When the next pair tried, one pony jumped but the other one stopped at the fence. He would not jump. After that several ponies jumped well, but none of them stayed side by side.

Then it was Billy and Tommy's turn. Dusty galloped beside Blaze and they jumped right together all the way around. Everybody clapped and cheered.

And when they rode home together Billy and Tommy each had a beautiful silver cup and each pony had a blue ribbon on its bridle. No boys were ever happier or prouder of their ponies.

Don't miss any of
Billy and Blazes adventures!

BILLY AND BLAZE
A BOY AND HIS PONY
BY C. W. ANDERSON

BLAZE AND THE FOREST FIRE
BILLY AND BLAZE SPREAD THE ALARM
BY C. W. ANDERSON

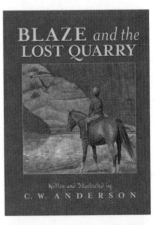

BLAZE and the LOST QUARRY
Written and Illustrated by
C. W. ANDERSON

BLAZE AND THE MOUNTAIN LION
BILLY AND BLAZE TO THE RESCUE
BY C. W. ANDERSON

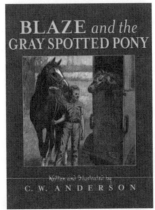

BLAZE and the GRAY SPOTTED PONY
Written and Illustrated by
C. W. ANDERSON

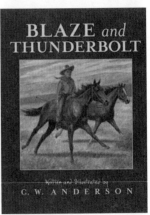

BLAZE and THUNDERBOLT
Written and Illustrated by
C. W. ANDERSON

BLAZE FINDS the TRAIL
Written and Illustrated by
C. W. ANDERSON

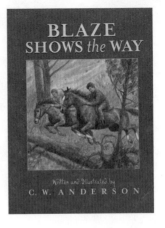

BLAZE SHOWS the WAY
Written and Illustrated by
C. W. ANDERSON